To William
Happy Christmas
CU00842003

For Beth, Jamie and Matt, not forgetting Sophia and Josh, and of course Matt and Krystle, but especially for Siân, with love ~ R.D.

To Karen, my wife, who always makes Christmas so special ~ D.F.

First published in 2012 by Pont Books, an imprint of
Gomer Press, Llandysul, Ceredigion, SA44 4JL
www.gomer.co.uk

ISBN 978 1 84851 386 0

A CIP record for this title is available from the British Library.

This book is published with the financial support of the
Welsh Books Council.

Printed and bound in Wales at Gomer Press,
Llandysul, Ceredigion

A Very Berry Christmas

David FitzGerald • Robert Dudley

Pont

It was just before Christmas.

All over Wales the snow had been falling.

At Tŷ Penbryn the garden lay under a thick white blanket of snow.

‘No gardening today, Meg,’ said Mr Hedges. ‘But the birds still need feeding.’

In the garden the snow was very deep. 'This is hard work,' said Mr Hedges as his boots sank deeper and deeper. But Meg loved it. She jumped in and out of the snow.

As Mr Hedges turned the corner, he saw a friend.

'Good morning,' he said. '*Bore da, Robin Goch*. Are you hungry for your breakfast? I've some seeds in my pocket . . . but you'll have to share them with the others.'

Meg watched Mr Hedges scatter birdseed on the crisp white snow.

'We'll break the ice on the birdbath,' he said, 'so the little birds can have a drink.'

Soon Meg was cold. She wanted to go back in the house and warm her paws.

'Come on,' said Mr Hedges. 'The birds are fed. Let's go indoors.'

Inside it was warm and cosy.
But outside the snow fell even faster.

Next day the snow was deeper still. All the roads were blocked.

'Oh dear,' said Mr Hedges. 'More snow. I don't think we'll be having a tree this Christmas.'

Every year he and Meg would choose a tree from the village . . .

and put it in the hall to decorate.

'It just won't be the same this Christmas,'
said Mr Hedges sadly. But then he had an idea . . .

He went up into the attic . . . and found the box of decorations.

'We'll have our Christmas tree outside,' he said.

Mr Hedges chose a tree and set to work.

He was busy all afternoon.

But somehow his tree just didn't look right.

'Oh dear,' he said. 'Even the star looks wonky. Come on, Meg. Let's go back inside.'

But the robin had been watching. He landed on a branch with a small red berry in his beak.

His friend the thrush was watching from the guttering, where icicles had frozen hard.

Suddenly the sky was filled with birds.
Each of them brought a gift for the tree.

As the sun set on Christmas Eve, the birds had finished their work.

Next morning Mr Hedges woke early. 'It's Christmas Day,' he said. 'I wonder if the snow has stopped.'

He pulled the curtain wide . . . and gasped.

‘Meg, come and look at this!’

'That's the most beautiful tree I've ever seen!' said Mr Hedges. 'Someone's been very busy. Look at all the tiny berries, Meg. And the little sprigs of holly. And the feathers . . . and the icicles.

Who has made our Christmas tree so special?’

We know who it was, don't we?

Nadolig Llawen, Mr Hedges!

A very berry Christmas!